Twenty-six Princesses

DAVE HOROWITZ

G. P. Putnam's Sons

For my brother, Rob

BIBLIOGRAPHY: Dunkling, Leslie, and William Gosling. *The New American Dictionary of Baby Names*. New York: Signet, 1983.

G. P. PUTNAM'S SONS ✴ A division of Penguin Young Readers Group. ✴ Published by The Penguin Group. ✴ Penguin Group (USA) Inc., 375 Hudson Street, New York, NY 10014, U.S.A. ✴ Penguin Group (Canada), 90 Eglinton Avenue East, Suite 700, Toronto, Ontario M4P 2Y3, Canada (a division of Pearson Penguin Canada Inc.). ✴ Penguin Books Ltd, 80 Strand, London WC2R 0RL, England. ✴ Penguin Ireland, 25 St. Stephen's Green, Dublin 2, Ireland (a division of Penguin Books Ltd.). ✴ Penguin Group (Australia), 250 Camberwell Road, Camberwell, Victoria 3124, Australia (a division of Pearson Australia Group Pty Ltd). ✴ Penguin Books India Pvt Ltd, 11 Community Centre, Panchsheel Park, New Delhi - 110 017, India. ✴ Penguin Group (NZ), 67 Apollo Drive, Rosedale, North Shore 0745, Auckland, New Zealand (a division of Pearson New Zealand Ltd.). ✴ Penguin Books (South Africa) (Pty) Ltd, 24 Sturdee Avenue, Rosebank, Johannesburg 2196, South Africa. ✴ Penguin Books Ltd, Registered Offices: 80 Strand, London WC2R 0RL, England.

Library of Congress Cataloging-in-Publication Data

Horowitz, Dave, 1970– Twenty-six princesses / Dave Horowitz. p. cm. Summary: Twenty-six princesses, one for each letter of the alphabet, go to a party at the prince's castle. Includes bibliographical references (p.2). [1. Princesses—Fiction. 2. Balls (Parties)—Fiction. 3. Alphabet. 4. Stories in rhyme.] I. Title. PZ8.3.H7848Tw 2008 [E]—dc22
2007013233   ISBN 978-0-399-24607-4   Special Markets ISBN 978-0-399-25269-3 Not for Resale   1 3 5 7 9 10 8 6 4 2

This Imagination Library edition is published by Penguin Group (USA), a Pearson company, exclusively for Dolly Parton's Imagination Library, a not-for-profit program designed to inspire a love of reading and learning, sponsored in part by The Dollywood Foundation. Penguin's trade editions of this work are available wherever books are sold.

Princess Alice. First to the palace.

Princess Betty. Still getting ready.

Princess **Criss**. Stealing a kiss.

Princess Dot. A lady she's not.

Princess Elle, Starting to yell.

Princess Flo. Waiting to go.

Princess **Grace**. Making a face.

Princess **Heather**. Dressed for the weather.

Princess Isabella. Has no umbrella.

Princess Jane. Being a pain.

Princess **Kay**. Lost her way.

Princess Lori. Not in this story.

Princess **Mandy**. Ate too much candy.

Princess Nell, What is that smell?

Princess Olga. Dancing the polka.

Princess Pearl, The littlest girl.

Princess **Quinn**. Doesn't fit in.

Princess Ruth. Mithing a tooth.

Princess Sue, Not you, too!

Princess Tess. Couldn't care less.

Princess Vikki. Very tricky.

Princess **Winnie**. Being a ninny.

Princess Xena. A true ballerina.

Princess **Yvette**. Isn't one, yet.

Princess Zaire. Finally there.

Put 'em all together
and what do you get?

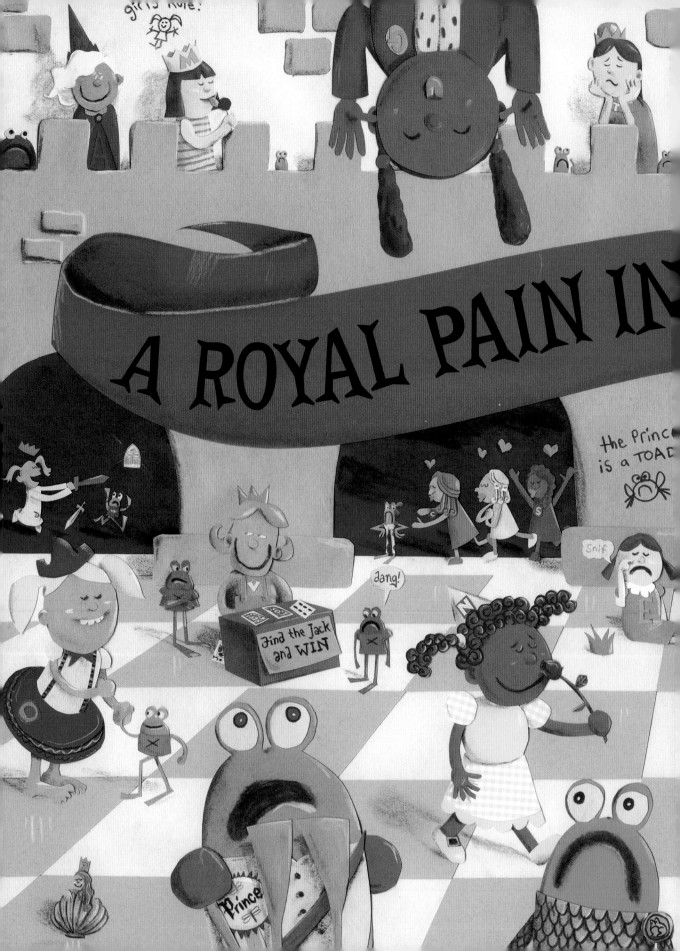

The End.